# Fire Engine is Flashing

Mandy Archer

Illustrated by Martha Lightfoot

NB

NEW BURLINGTON

The sun rises over the fire station.
Fire Engine waits behind the big red doors.

It is very quiet. Upstairs, the crew are sleeping.

Only Fox keeps one eye open.

The fire alarm starts r<sub>i</sub>ng<sub>i</sub>ng.

BBBRRRRRIIIINNG!

Fox leaps out of bed.

Firefighters rush
to pull on **boots**
and buckle up **coats**.

Fox is first to **slide**
down the pole.

Fire Engine is ready to **go!**

Hurry, **hurry!**

Fox grabs his **helmet** and
climbs into the **driver's cab.**

Fox flicks **switches** and pulls **levers**.

Fire Engine's motor
starts to **rumble**
and
**shake.**

The fire station doors **spring open**.
Lights shine **bright**.

**VROOM!**
VROOM!

Fire Engine **zooms** out.
This is an **emergency!**

The **Commander** speaks to Fox on the radio.

NEE-NAW!
NEE-NAW!

There's a **fire** blazing in an apartment block! Fire Engine goes even **faster**.

Fire Engine **screeches** to a stop outside the apartment block.

**Flames** lick the building and **smoke** billows out.

Fox quickly **unrolls** Fire Engine's **hose.**

Fox finds a hydrant and connects up the hose.

WWOOOSHH!

A jet of water hits the flames.

The Commander's car pulls up.

He points to the top floor - somebody is stuck inside!

The crew unfold Fire Engine's **ladder**. There's not a second to lose!

Fox puts on his **mask** and **air-tank**. The smoke will make it hard to breathe.

Fox **climbs** to the top of the **ladder**.

It is **very hot** and there is lots of **smoke**.

CRACKLE!

CRACKLE!

The **police** hold everyone back to keep them safe.

A **lady waves** from the top-floor **window.**

It will be difficult
to reach her.

Fire Engine needs
to move **closer.**

Fire Engine **edges** back
a bit. The ladder goes
**up** again.

Now Fox can reach!

He carefully **breaks** the **glass**
and carries the lady out.

The crowd give a **big cheer!**

When the last flame has gone out,
the **firefighters** put away their
**tools** and wind up the hose.

# Let's look at
# Fire Engine

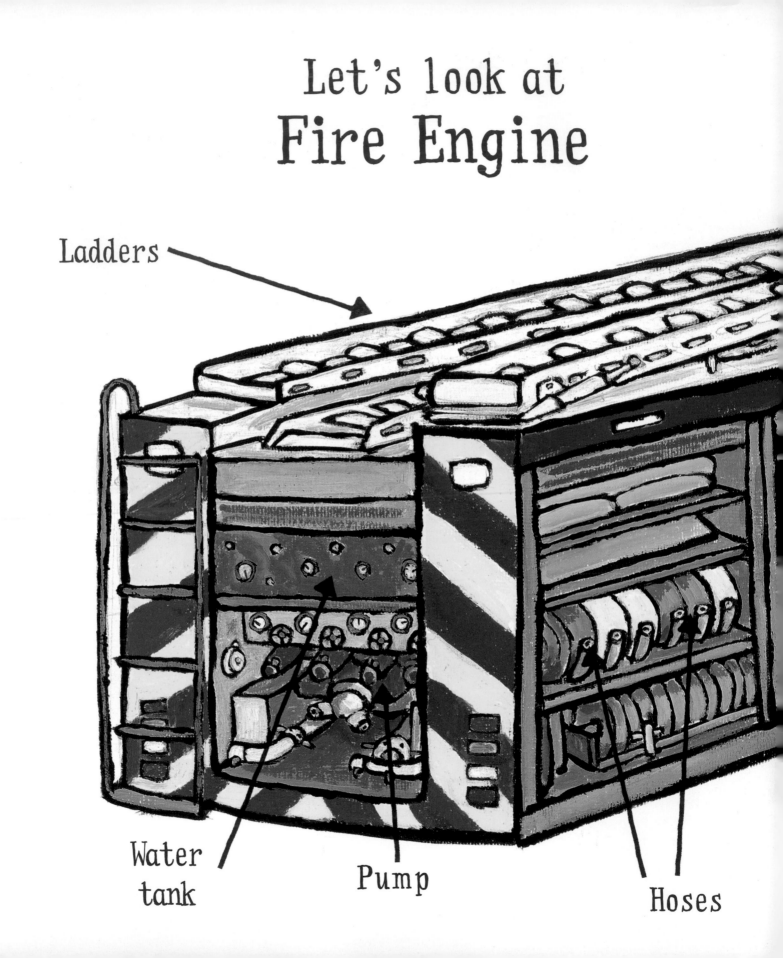

Ladders

Water
tank

Pump

Hoses

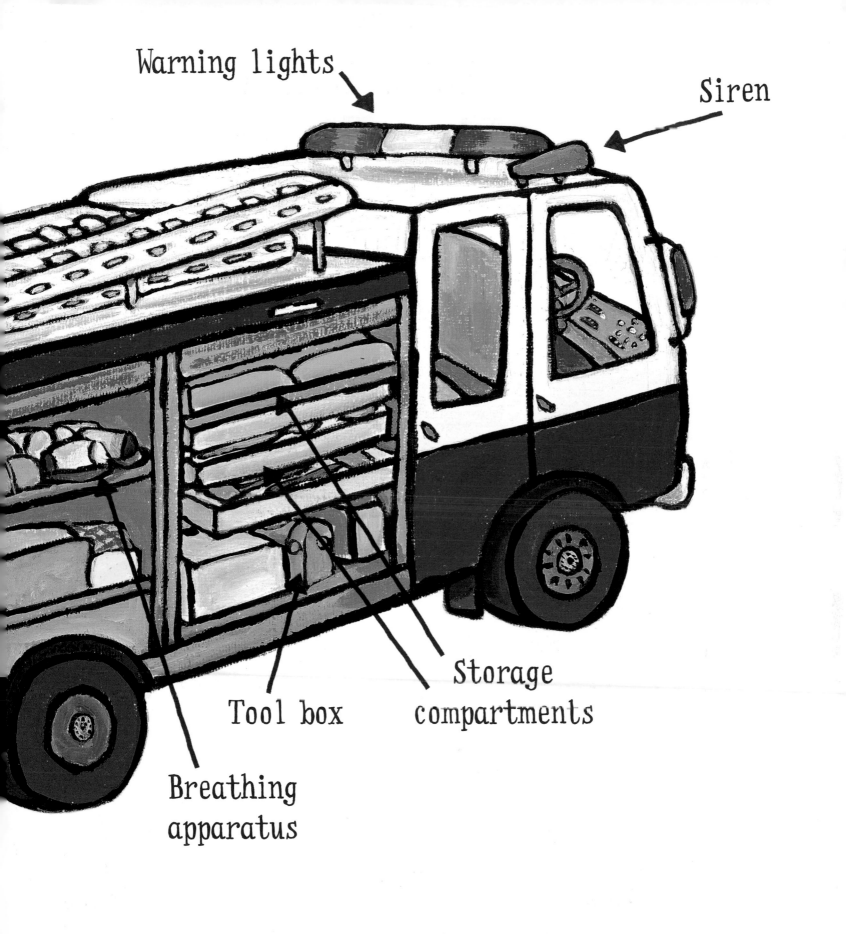

Warning lights

Siren

Breathing
apparatus

Tool box

Storage
compartments

# Other Emergency Machines

## Police car

## Fire bike

# Ambulance

# Commander's car

For Tamar M. L.

A NEW BURLINGTON BOOK
The Old Brewery
6 Blundell Street
London N7 9BH

Designer: Plum Pudding Design

Copyright © QED Publishing 2012

First published in hardback in the UK in 2012 by
QED Publishing
Part of The Quarto Group
The Old Brewery, 6 Blundell Street
London, N7 9BH

A catalogue record for this book is available from the British Library.

ISBN: 978 1 78171 049 4

Printed in China